# THE DIARY OF
# ARCHIE THE ALPACA

# THE DIARY OF
# ARCHIE the ALPACA

*with*

## KEVIN MacNEIL

*Illustrated by* Moose Allain

Polygon

First published in Great Britain in 2017 by
Polygon, an imprint of Birlinn Ltd
West Newington House
10 Newington Road
Edinburgh EH9 1QS

www.polygonbooks.co.uk

9 8 7 6 5 4 3 2 1

ISBN  978 1 84697 406 9
eBook ISBN 978 0 85790 981 7

*British Library Cataloguing-in-Publication Data.* A catalogue record for
this book is available on request from the British Library.

Designed by Teresa Monachino
Printed and bound in the EU by Scandbook

*Dedicated to alpaca rights*

# FOREWORD

Some readers are doubtless acquainted with my late friend, Archie the Alpaca. I have documented his adventures in *The Brilliant & Forever*. For those unaware of him, all I can say is: what an alpaca he was. He loved writing, dancing, using his spittoon, and carousing. He adored his two cats, Katsu and Kimi.

Following Archie's departure from this life I found a diary he kept and a note asking that I publish it. 'What use,' he wrote, 'is a secret diary if you don't publish it.'

His diary referenced pieces of prose and poetry he wrote – and subsequently hid – so I would need to find them before offering them for publication. As I sorted through his possessions I found more and more items Archie had written and alluded to in his diary.

In an apparently empty coffee jar there was a rolled-up piece of paper with a short story on it.

I found a radio sketch in a biscuit tin ('I hope people read this with the right voices in their head').

I found a poem written on the back of garish, peeling wallpaper, and some haiku encoded in a notebook apparently dedicated to Archie's reviews of the true crime shows he loved.

Finally I found a postdated email in my junk file, typed by Archie before his predicted demise. It asked me to seek the advice of Neville Moir, Joanna Swainson, Francis, Vikki, and Young Flossy. 'They'll know better than you, Kevin; my writing's a jazz thing *you* don't get.'

KEVIN MacNEIL

# LAST DAY
## OF THE
# PREVIOUS YEAR

Two dangers exist on the road of truth, a wise man once said – not starting and not going all the way.

I have kept this book short.

Dali imagined a world where time was soft.
But now times are hard for Surrealists everywhere.

THE DIARY OF
ARCHIE the ALPACA

January

Open your eyes like the sun rising.

There are so many people in the world that the chances of someone breathing in unison with you right now are very high indeed. Feel synchronised.

Quiet coach, train to London.
Someone has a SatNav.
'In 300 metres, turn left.'

Salvador Dali said: 'Every morning when I wake up, I feel an exquisite sense of joy – the joy of being Salvador Dali. And I ask myself, in a sort of rapture, what wonderful thing will he create today, this Salvador Dali!' I wish he were alive today to post this on social media.

## AFTER MY CAT ATE A TIN OF MACKEREL AND
## CHICKEN BREAST CAT FOOD


*Elphie (neighbour cat):* Yo, Katsu, your breath smells weird.

*Katsu (my cat):* What – no, it's just mackerel and chicken breast.

*Elphie:* Mackerel and what-now?

Katsu launches into an epic tale of how he had a massive once-in-nine-lifetimes fight, on a farm by a river, with a fish and a chicken simultaneously, ending in his seizing the mackerel in one paw and the chicken in the other, before devouring them both like the miniature lion he is.

    Yes, Katsu. But you and I know the truth. You and I know the truth.

There's no need to kill time.
It takes time to learn that time is a knife that heals.

Edited my pants and socks drawer in the morning, now doing the same to a screenplay.

sunlight on the loch
the fence trembling;
her hand on my shoulder

## SITTING IN THE NIGHINTGALE WITH TOOTHACHE CAFE

I spoon some sugar into my shimmering grassuccino and stir. I wonder about all the individuals who were involved in bringing this grassuccino and this sugar to this table, all these solid little miracles being what they are, in their allotted place. They will fade. This cafe will fade. You yourself will fade. Life has a fading nature. Sensitivity makes noise of us all.

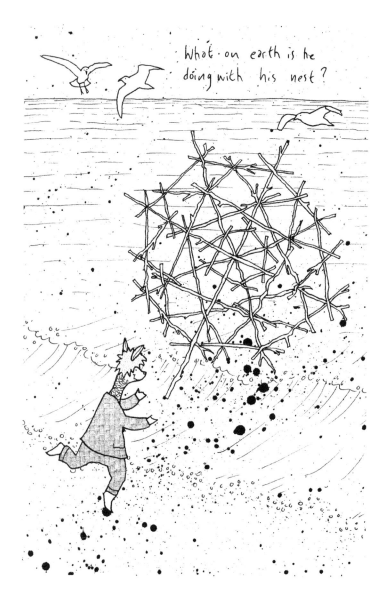

THE DIARY OF
**ARCHIE** THE **ALPACA**

February

Collect driftwood, make art-pieces, throw them back.

Sleepily hallucinated that a film director, a piper, a director of photography and the daughter of a South American missionary were in the living room watching Irish hip-hop videos on YouTube. Went through to the living room and right enough, it was really happening.

Mime your innocence to a CCTV camera.

'Now can you see the screen?'
'Yes. Nice cinema. Good leg room.'
'We're in the front row.'

Visit an art gallery.

Take home themes from your own life.

I was a happy, relaxed and popular alpaca in primary school. Those days were bright yellow with joy, I was bookish and sporty, ideas flew through my mind like a soaring shot on goal.

Sometimes the North Atlantic wind whipped the ball away, like God was on the other team.

My friends and I were skinny, energetic, polite, safe. The golden days were often punctuated by a bird's poignant call, the elegiac melody of the wood pigeon. To this day, every time I hear a wood pigeon, my heart physically pangs. I wanted to be a famous footballer who could score the winning goal with a header even after all his legs were broken in a mysterious incident on the pitch earlier and also I yearned to be a writer who could compose poems that had the same impact on others the wood pigeon's song had on me.

Repeat things only when you must. (Repeat things.)

## MY NEW NOVEL

My new novel is a deconstructed novel. You get a dictionary, notebook, pen and a pair of glasses (without any lenses).

Take your time, old chap. I'm all ears.

THE DIARY OF
ARCHIE THE ALPACA

March

Obliterate sarcasm with a healthy chuckle.

We all know Edinburgh's Waverley Station is named after the Walter Scott novels, but did you know that Grand Central Station is named after Elizabeth Smart's beautiful novella *By Grand Central Station I Sat Down and Wept*?

Put a shell to your ear and you hear the sea;
touch noses with a cat and you smell cat food.

that dog on the train
could be a human being
barking at time's heels

Sauntered into Tiffany's whistling Moon River, put on my best Truman Capote accent, asked if their breakfasts are all-day, got chucked out.

The finest phrase in the English language:
'Oh, and I bought you a custard slice.'

Above all, a stunning moon, one which is not quite the same as any a not-quite-the-same-you has ever seen.

writing haiku late
into the night i forgot
to put the clock forward

WHAT I LEARNED FROM MY FRIEND'S TALKING TORTOISE:

Take things at your own pace.
Your life continues when other lives are gone;
other lives continue when yours is gone.
Soft interior. Hard exterior.
Plan ahead.
Cultivate patient, endurance.
Always have a haven.

*Dentist:* Any plans for the weekend?

*Me:* I'm going to do couple of big bike rides.

*Dentist:* No, you're not.

*Me* (frowning): Is the forecast bad?

*Dentist* (laughing): No.

THE DIARY OF
ARCHIE THE ALPACA

April

Write your own elegy, code it and
bury it in the text of your will.

Also good for the ego is being rejected by a magazine you didn't send work to. Magazine, I reject your rejection, just as I reject your policy of rejecting material that is unrejectable by virtue of its never being submitted in the first place.

Thought I'd happily get through life without buying an angle grinder. I was wrong.

Visited the excellent Museum of Transport in Glasgow. Semi-invented a genre, The Found Lydia Davis Story. Under the Sinclair C5 battery powered car is a card that reads: 'I won this C5 in a competition. Everyone came out to see me drive it – I felt like the Pied Piper. It was useless on hills.'

What we read is the quality of our reading.

writing a love letter
too quickly, i upset
my cup of green tea

THE DIARY OF
ARCHIE THE ALPACA

May

Sometimes short stories are what happen
when you're busy making other novels.

Unexpectedly bumped into Kim Jong-un in the Bentall's Centre, Kingston. He looked a bit sheepish and chuckled as he said, 'I'm just on holiday, it's no biggie. This is the last place they'd expect to find me. I don't think the average person realises how exhausting it is being a despot.' I asked him how he's filling his days and he told me he's reading *A Girl is a Half-Formed Thing* and watching a Laurel and Hardy box-set.

Unusually for a cat, Katsu chases anyone on a bicycle. Following a horrendous near-miss, no option now but to lock away Katsu's bike.

AT A BUDDHIST PROTEST:

'What do we want?'
'An end to desire!'
'When do we want it?'
'We don't.'

Cycled, made sushi, wrote some recipes, started drafting a book review. Oh yeah, and some scientists discovered an alien megastructure.

What will the alien megastructure make of kittens?
That is the real question.

THE DIARY OF
ARCHIE THE ALPACA

June

Indulge in diversions.
Throw away the road map.

## MOBILE PHONES IN PUBLIC PLACES

When people lower their voice to say, 'I love you too, snugglebum, bye' ... why couldn't they have conducted their whole conversation at that volume?

A warm hug is a comfort.

Though admittedly yes, less so, officer, when it's a case of mistaken identity.

Sanctify a place no one else holds dear.

by the gravestone
two cats, ballet-like,
boxing

Visited Mary Shelley's grave, Bournemouth. It's also the burial place of Percy Bysshe Shelley's heart, following his largely but not wholly successful cremation in Italy.

I believe we may be witnessing an extinction level event.

THE DIARY OF
ARCHIE THE ALPACA

July

Rearrange your diary. Begin the year with July.

Eating out. 100% certain the waiter is an English guy putting on a French accent. He is, whether actually or in character, struggling to understand my Hebridean accent.

over the Colosseum
as over a blackhouse
the moon in its moon-ness

ONCE, IN GALWAY CITY

You have to love Ireland; it's fond of literature and kind to alpacas. Once, in Galway City, I was sharing a room with an Irishman, with two beds, two bedside tables, two lamps. It was dark. We had turned in for the night. Suddenly, the Irishman sat upright, turned his light on and scribbled a few lines of poetry on a piece of paper. 'Sorry about that,' he said as he switched off the light and settled back. 'I just had a muse flash'.

## SLEEP

Sleep, sleep, sleep … like so many things in life, I love you without telling you. What in the world made you think you should be my enemy?

Refresh me now, or I'll killyougoddamnit.

two boys scream
in the waiting room and hurl
dinosaurs at each other

## COLIN THE COCKROACH

As Colin the Cockroach awoke one morning from uneasy dreams he found himself transformed in his bed into a tiny Kafka.

Refused to watch the Ford Madox Ford programme at nine thirty; will tune in at nine thirty-nine as he would've wanted.

Star-matter in the
physical sky, star-matter
in the heart. Sunrise.

Wow. Just saw Gravity in 3D at the IMAX. Amazing. Left the cinema truly believing in gravity.

Someone laced his drinks a little too tight.

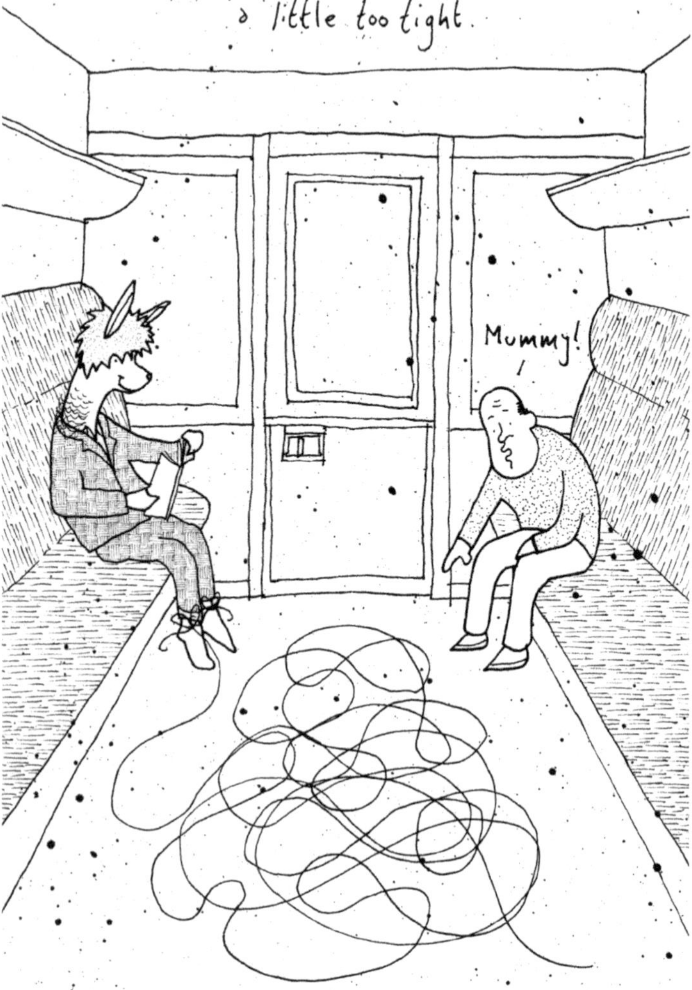

THE DIARY OF
ARCHIE THE ALPACA

August

Campaign to protect an endangered species –
The ugliest one you can find.

(Pointing to vehicle in front)
'Look, a combine harvester!'
'That's a bin lorry.'
'I know, I romanticised it into a combine harvester since we're in the West Country.'

Read a short story by 'Bradford's Chekhov'.
Now I want to read something by:
'Edinburgh's Ryunosuke Akutagawa';
'Lochboisdale's Alice Munro';
'Manhattan's Sorley MacLean'.

Dear god, how many alpaca-hours have I wasted on Facebook? Anyway, I wrote a poem.

> They know what he eats for breakfast
> And how much he craves 'likes'.
> They've seen his holiday
> photos, since he befriended
> them on Facebook, that poet,
> but if their lives depended on it, they
> could not quote a line he wrote.

'Bye, have a good weekend.'
Thank the lord I've so little money for
them not to look after.

Not saying the man opposite me on the train is drunk,
but he is staring hard, trying to understand
my shoelaces.

Searches people made which took them to my website: 'avoid evil'; 'the speaker is death'; 'isle of lewis what is it like'; 'it's gonna hurt'; 'astonished open mouth'.

in the East End, a kitten
crosses the street
with a swagger

a wet crow cackles
above the gloomy airport
I've lost my passport

darkness gathering
even the beggar's 'any change?'
seems ominous

No white horses today, my friend

THE DIARY OF
ARCHIE THE ALPACA

September

Here, of all places, right now – you.
You who once set out naked and daft.

Remembering Dali. 'Every morning when I wake up, I feel a terrible sense of nothingness – the nothingness of being Archie the Alpaca. And I ask myself, in a sort of paralysis, what failed thing will he create today, this Archie the Alpaca.'

## AS IF

As if I intermittently had too much happiness, much of it undeserved, and the overflow of joy came splashing over the edges of my senses, like golden wine, 'bottled poetry', for example when reading to an amphitheatre(!) of poetry fans, or realising the first touch of her smile, fulfilment incarnate, only it was always imbued with the residue of insecurity, as if life's wine, so happily nourished by sunshine and soil, had corked altogether, grown bitter to itself, and now thirsted for a new beginning, also undeserved.

Opening soon – Zeitgeist: the bespoke steampunk burlesque erotic fiction bakery college.

You can take a seahorse to water.

a white ambulance
flies, lights flashing like wings, fierce,
racing the angels

*Throws iPad and keyboard across the room in such a way they land neatly in their respective protective bags*
*Leaps out of chair, does a double backflip, lands on feet like a ninja*
*Clicks fingers, announces, 'I'm outta here.'*
*Grins, winks at camera*
*Turns away, mutters to self grimly, 'Because I'm spending the weekend cleaning the kitchen.'*

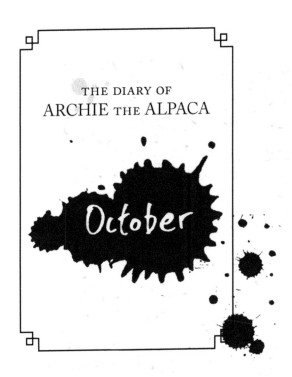

THE DIARY OF
**ARCHIE** THE **ALPACA**

*October*

Experiment with your social skills.

One of my neighbours stopped me in the street to say that he's moving house today and he made a long, emotional farewell speech, and asked if we could swap phone numbers, then at the end of his speech he asked me what my name was.

Bruges. Sugar overdose. A bus tour whose audio guide recording is seventy percent music as there just isn't that much to say about Bruges. A taxi driver who arrives ten minutes early so he has someone to talk to. A fine place to spend two and a quarter days. Especially if you like chocolate, waffles the size of a mattress, churches, chocolate, and hot chocolate.

You are already adequately equipped.

THE DIARY OF
ARCHIE THE ALPACA

November

It's a brilliant moon,
Earth's.

Met a guy in Kingston whose grandfather was a Hearach (Harrisman) who worked as a police officer in Glasgow. He'd stride into the pubs in Maryhill, all six-foot-three of him, with his fifty-six inch chest, held a hand up to get everyone's attention then say in a gentle lilt: 'It's getting rowdy in here. If you don't quieten down I'll come round and punch you all individually.' There was a man who knew how to use an adverb.

Bought a used book about Zen. The previous owner had already written my notes in it.

Loneliness. Even the moon
is gone. Sitting here thinking –
another peat on the fire?

Next time I grudge paying rail fares, which are extortionate, remind me that at least I often get a story out of the journey. This time it was a man who was travelling in first-class while his wife and kids travelled in a standard class carriage(!) He came through to the 'quiet' coach to berate them because they ignored/missed a text he sent telling the wife to get the daughter to bring him a certain newspaper (which the wife was reading); mister first-class was going to pay the daughter £2 to bring the paper to him.

Now that's a first-class-first-world-problem.

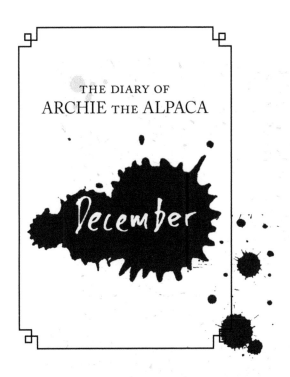

THE DIARY OF
**ARCHIE** THE **ALPACA**

*December*

Appreciate brief longings.

So after all the hype I cracked and went to the cinema to see the latest Star Wars movie. I loved the look of the film, the soundtrack. The nuanced performances, the great clothes, the cool 1950s spacecraft. I was surprised when it got a bit raunchy. Wait, not Star Wars – Carol. I saw the film Carol.

Send a letter of thanks (or commiseration)
to someone who has influenced you.

under icy stars
a cow's indignant 'moo!'
answers my 'here, kitty kitty.'

Glaswegian woman on train describing large Christmas tree 'with 150 lights on it, lit up like a Las Vegas hoorhoose.'

EJECTED FROM LONDON, THIS ALPACA HOPPED
A TRAIN TO CAITHNESS:

Every few miles, a house;
the train rushes on
through loneliness.

## EVERY WINTER, PERHAPS FOREVER

Every Winter I find myself reading about ghosts, feeling strangely more empty, possibly turning into one.

Six deadlines fast approaching. Head pounding. Ireland goes into economic tailspin. Glasgow becomes more dangerous than Kabul. London follows suit. Sleep becomes a luxury, not a right. Inbox (167) and ringing of phone become portentous. Somebody walks off a stage or out of a jungle or into an engagement. Santa beckons, cheaply glittering in the shadows; 'Lend us a fiver?'

It is *the* story of our times. A woman joins a search party looking for herself.

Farewell, Dali. 'Every morning when I wake up, I feel an inarguable sense of equanimity – the equanimity of being Archie the Alpaca. And I ask myself, in a state of gratitude, what changing things today shall bring, to the changing world and to the changing part of it temporarily known as Archie the Alpaca.'

Kitten's asleep in her little bed beside me while I hammer away at the new novel, she in her world, I in mine. And yet us in ours. Perfect.

ACKNOWLEDGEMENTS:

*Be Wise Be Otherwise* (Canongate), *New Writing
Scotland* (ASLS), Less is More or Less More, *404 Ink:
Error, Anthology.*

Moose Allain; Neville Moir, Vikki Reilly, Alison Rae,
Edward Crossan, James Hutcheson and everyone at
Polygon; Katsu and Kimi; Young Flossy; my colleagues
at the University of Stirling; Francis; Innes; Mathy;
Akutagawa.

KEVIN MACNEIL is a leading Scottish novelist, poet, screenwriter and playwright, born and raised in the Outer Hebrides. His most recent novel, *The Brilliant & Forever*, was published to huge critical acclaim and was shortlisted for the Saltire Fiction of the Year Award in 2016. He recently edited *Robert Louis Stevenson: An Anthology, Selected by Jorge Luis Borges & Adolfo Bioy Casares*. Kevin has won a number of prestigious literary award and lectures on the Creative Writing course at the University of Stirling.

MOOSE ALLAIN is an artist, illustrator and prolific tweeter. His cartoons feature regularly in the *Literary Review* and *Private Eye* magazines. His illustration projects range from an exhibition guide for Tate Britain, *The A-Z of Pointless*, to a variety of murals for a waxing salon in Mexico City. He lives and works in Devon.